The Magic Knot
~ and other tangles!

&

The Tale of None

© Copyright 2007 Reg Down

All rights reserved. No part of this book may be reproduced in any form or by any means without the written prior permission of the author, except for brief quotations embodied in critical articles for review.

Book sales in USA (only):

LIGHTLY PRESS
4033 San Juan Ave. #219
Fair Oaks
CA 95628
regdown@hotmail.com

~ Other Children's Books by Reg Down ~

The Tales of Tiptoes Lightly
The Bee who Lost his Buzz
Pumpkin Crow
Lucy Goose and the Half-egg

The Festival of Stones
Autumn and Winter Tales of Tiptoes Lightly

Big-Stamp Two-Toes the Barefoot Giant
Spring Tales of Tiptoes Lightly

The Lost Lagoon
Adventures of Tiptoes Lightly and Greenleaf the Sailor

***

~ Praise for Tiptoes Lightly and her Stories ~

"*Renewal: The Journal for Waldorf Education* doesn't usually publish stories. But children in Waldorf Schools are nourished every day by stories, and we adults, too, need a story now and then, especially one that inspires wonder and joy at nature and stimulates our imaginative capacity for forming inner pictures. So here is a little tale about a fairy named Tiptoes Lightly, who lives in an acorn at the top of a great oak tree…"

Ronald Koetzsch, Ph.D — Editor
Renewal – The Journal for Waldorf Education

"Our preschooler hasn't been a big chapter-book fan, but she routinely asked for another Tiptoes Story. Borrow or Buy?: Buy! It's a great way to introduce the chapter book concept to young readers and will be a book that middle-readers will enjoy a second (or third) time around."

The Reading Tub Review

"My children were enchanted by Pine Cone and Pepper Pot's adventures in preparation for Tiptoes' special birthday party!"
Sonya Bingaman — owner of 'A Toy Garden'

"I read these stories to the children in my class every week for a whole year – they loved them! Their faces shone with obvious delight – I recommend them highly."
Miki Higashine — grade school teacher

"For five years the children in my kindergarten delighted in experiencing the adventures of Tiptoes and her many friends. These tales are filled with wonder, magic and joy."
Susan Rice – kindergarten teacher

"Reg Down has created a magical world where children can be nurtured through storytelling."
Margarita Cervantes — kindergarten teacher

"I've fallen in love with Tiptoes."
Donella Jean – mother of two

A wonderful book for children! We got this book (The Tales of Tiptoes Lightly) when our daughter was three. Now that she is four, she continues to love the stories in this trilogy and asks for them every night before bed. They are wonderfully written and short, making them well-suited for an evening bedtime story."
David Eichler — Amazon reviewer

"Thank you so much for writing down Tiptoes' tales ... the book stays by my bedside and sends me off to peaceful sleep. The images and your sweet illustrations are joyful, fun and beautiful ..."
Katherine W. — artist and teacher

"My children and I LOVE your books! Thank you!"
Nancy W. — Oregon

"We have loved the first book, and the other two are currently in hiding, waiting for Valentine's Day. Thank you for the wonderful stories, and the inspiration!"
Karine Calhoun — artist

"My six year old and I discovered your books and are so delighted. We have a cast of 'characters' that live in our house and my son is sure that our 'Baby Mousie' is a cousin to Jeremy Mouse. Anyway, they all crowd in bed with us as we read these stories at night. We can't wait till your third collection of Tiptoes and Jeremy Mouse stories come out!!!"
Maica Belknap — California

"My grandson just loves your stories!"
Noel Brenner — California

"Your stories are so wonderfully written. Thank you so much for your first three books, my girls absolutely love them ..."
Carmencita Walsh — B.C., Canada

"Our customers love your books! A mom was in today telling how her children want your stories read every night. I recommend them without hesitation."
Valerie Hope — Steiner Storehouse, Portland, Oregon

"My children and I love this book, (it) is a favorite in our house. We have read and reread this book during bedtime. Reg also wrote another book about Tiptoes that we have and highly recommend."
C. Costa — Amazon reviewer

"I have to tell you I'm in love with Tiptoes Lightly. We will definitely be carrying it."
Debbie Staggs — owner of 'A Child's Dream Come True'

"Your books, that you left with me at the 'Spring Creek Store' in the Portland Waldorf School, sold like hotcakes!"
Rose Sable-Dodge

CONTENTS

THE MAGIC KNOT
AND OTHER TANGLES

1 — The House of Tiptoes Lightly 10
2 — One Table and Three Chairs 11
3 — Just the Right Branch 13
4 — The Gnomes are NOT speaking 16
5 — Snake or Elephant? 19
6 — The Branch is Not Good Food 24
7 — Dotty Owl 26
8 — The Table and Chairs are Drawn 29
9 — The Branch is Chewed 32
10 — Pepper Pot is Flyed 35
11 — Pepper Pot is Pulled 37
12 — Jeremy Mouse is Called 39
13 — Pepper Pot is Tree-Pulled 40
14 — Annoyetta is Found 43
15 — Pepper Pot is Snipped 47
16 — Wax is Thought of 48
17 — Two Fine and Handsome Sailors 50
18 — The Bees Wax Generous 55
19 — The Boot is Found 57
20 — Pepper Pot Sits Again 59
21 — Off to the Great Oak Tree 62
22 — The Chairs are Hauled 64

23 — *The Table is Not Hauled* 66
24 — *Ompliant Sort-of Helps* 70
25 — *Two Brave Gnomes and One Table* 73
26 — *The Knot Knots* 75
27 — *Tiptoes' Surprise* 79
28 — *More Visitors* 84
29 — *Tiptoes Tells how She was Born* 86
30 — *Tiptoes is Told the Truth* 89

***

The Tale of None 93

Author's Note 98

To my children
Aran, Oisin and Isa
— for all the stories we shared
when you were young.

The Magic Knot
~ *and other tangles!*

~ STARRING ~
Pine Cone and Pepper Pot
&
the lovely
Tiptoes Lightly

Written and illustrated
by
Reg Down

1
The House of Tiptoes Lightly

Tiptoes lives in a great oak tree—
inside an acorn as small as can be!
She has golden hair, bright yellow wings and a sky blue dress. Her house has one door to go in and out of, two windows to look in and out of, and one roof. Inside her house she has a feather bed made of two downy feathers. They were given to her specially by Lucy the Goose—one feather to lie down on, and one feather to cover her up. This keeps Tiptoes warm and she never gets cold at night, not even in wintertime. She also has a small, round table and three chairs. Her friends, Pine Cone and Pepper Pot the gnomes, made them for her birthday.

This is how they were made.

2
One Table and Three Chairs

Pine Cone and Pepper Pot are friends. Their house lies underneath the roots of an old pine tree, deep in the forest on Farmer John's land. They wear earthy green jackets and pants, and both have red boots with pointy, curling-up toes. They also have red caps that sparkle on top—especially when they are excited or have good ideas! Pine Cone loves honey and Pepper Pot loves pepper. Pepper Pot shakes so much pepper onto his food that it gets into his bushy beard. When you hug Pepper Pot you always sneeze!

"It's going to be Tiptoes' birthday soon," said Pine Cone to Pepper Pot one day. "We have to make her a present."

"What shall we make her?" asked Pepper Pot. "She doesn't need very much. Her house is just a teeny tiny acorn!"

"She needs a table," said Pine Cone. "She doesn't have a table."

"That's a good idea!" agreed Pepper Pot. "We'll make her a table."

"And a table needs a chair," said Pine Cone. "She doesn't have a chair."

"Yes," agreed Pepper Pot again, nodding his head up and down. "She must have a chair to sit at her table."

"But where will her visitors sit?" asked Pine Cone. "What will happen when Pins and Needles the house fairies visit? Or Twiglets and Spriglets the orchard fairies? Where will they sit?"

"Even Jeremy Mouse and Jemima Mouse," added Pepper Pot. "Even you and me!"

"Tiptoes must have three chairs," declared Pine Cone, the tip of his red cap glowing brightly. "One table and three chairs—that is what we shall make for her birthday!"

"I agree," said Pepper Pot, rubbing his hands together. "Let's get started right away—her birthday is very soon."

"First we need to find just the right branch from just the right tree," said Pine Cone. "The wood has to be perfect," and out of their house they went.

3
Just the Right Branch

Pine Cone and Pepper Pot went looking for the perfect branch. First they searched close to their house.

"Here's one!" called Pepper Pot excitedly. "I found a branch!"

"It's too green," said Pine Cone, looking at it carefully. "It has to be just the right age and perfectly dry."

So they went further into the forest and looked some more.

"Here's one!" cried Pepper Pot. "I found another!"

"It's too old," said Pine Cone. "See, the wood is already rotting away. Let's look over there," and he pointed to some trees far into the forest.

So off they trekked and searched some more.

"Here's another one!" hollered Pepper Pot, jumping up and down. "This one looks good!"

"Too soft," said Pine Cone, poking at it with a stick. "The branch has to have hard wood and not soft wood. We should go to the maple trees over there on yonder hill."

So they hiked deeper into the forest to the maple trees and looked some more.

"Here's one!" shouted Pepper Pot, pointing excitedly to a log.

"It's much too big," said Pine Cone when he saw it. "We'll never be able to pick it up. Let's try the next hill where the ash trees grow."

So they marched to the ash grove deep in the forest and looked some more.

"Here's a really good one!" cried Pepper Pot, doing a little dance. "This one looks perfect! I know it's perfect!"

"It *is* perfect!" declared Pine Cone as soon as he saw the branch. "It's just right ... but how are we to get it home? It's too far!"

"Too far! Too far!" grumped Pepper Pot, pulling off his red cap and waving it up and down in the air. "First it's too green, then its too old, or too soft, or too big! And now we've found the perfect branch and you say it's too far to bring home!" and he sat down on the ground in a huff.

Pine Cone scratched his head and pulled on his beard. "What are we to do?" he moaned. "What are we to do?"

4
The Gnomes are NOT Speaking

Pine Cone and Pepper Pot sat in the forest for a long time. Pepper Pot was grumpy with Pine Cone because he was so fussy about getting just the right branch. And Pine Cone was grumpy with Pepper Pot because Pepper Pot was grumpy. It wasn't his fault that the perfect piece of wood was much too far from home. They sat back to back on the ground and were not speaking to each other.

"I'm *not* speaking to you," grumped Pepper Pot, sticking his nose in the air.

"And I'm not speaking to you *either*!" replied Pine Cone, sticking his nose even higher.

"Well, I'm not even listening to you," said Pepper Pot.

"And I'm certainly not listening to you," retorted Pine Cone.

"That's because you're such a ninny goose," said Pepper Pot.

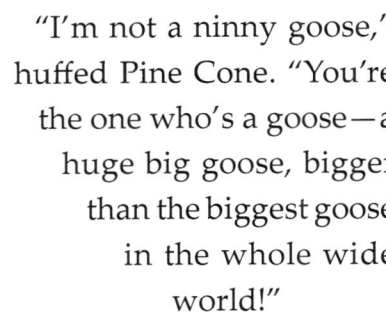

"I'm not a ninny goose," huffed Pine Cone. "You're the one who's a goose—a huge big goose, bigger than the biggest goose in the whole wide world!"

"You're the most biggerest goose of all," said Pepper Pot, " and now I'm *really* not talking to you!"

Pine Cone and Pepper Pot spent a long time not talking to each other!

Suddenly they heard leaves and twigs crunching and crackling! Louder and louder, step by step the noises came towards them through the forest. Trees and branches swayed back and forth and the ground began to shake. Then a huge head looked around a tree trunk, and said: "Hoo-humpf! What's this? Two grumpy gnomes?"

"It's Ompliant the Elephant!" cried the gnomes, jumping up and hugging his trunk.

"Hoo-humpf!" said Ompliant. "My ears have been telling me things."

"What things?" asked Pine Cone and Pepper Pot, their ears perking up.

"They've been telling me about gnomes," replied Ompliant. "Arguing gnomes!" and he swished his skinny tail back and forth.

"You're right," cried Pine Cone and Pepper Pot. "That's us! We've been arguing!"

"Hoo-humpf! Is that so? What have you been arguing about?"

"We're making one table and three chairs for Tiptoes' birthday,"

explained Pine Cone, "and we've found the perfect branch to make them."

"That's good!" said Ompliant. "So why are you arguing?"

"The branch is too big! And it's much too far for little folk like us to carry home," said Pepper Pot unhappily. "What are we to do?"

Ompliant flapped his ears back and forth and thought hard.

"I don't know," he said at last. "Let's ask Mr. Beaver. He knows about wood," and off they went.

5
Snake or Elephant?

Ompliant the Elephant and the gnomes went marching through the forest towards Soggy Mire where Mr. Beaver lived. It was a long way, but at last the ground became soft and wet and Ompliant had to put the gnomes onto his back. Soon he was sinking into muddy water up to his tummy, but he kept on going until he reached the House of Beaver. Beaver's lodge was a huge pile of mud and sticks sitting half in and half out of the water.

"Yoo-hoo!" cried Pine Cone and Pepper Pot as loudly as they could. "Yoo-hoo, Mr. Beaver!"

But there was no reply.

"Yoo-hoo! Yoo-hoo!" they cried again—but no one came out.

"Maybe he can't hear you," said Ompliant. "He doesn't have a door like normal folk. His door is under the water."

"Stick your trunk inside his house," suggested Pine Cone. "It's plenty long enough."

So Ompliant stretched out his trunk, put it under the water and found the door. Then he stuck it into Beaver's house.

"Yoooo-hoooo! Yoooo-hoooo!" he called. "Is anyone ho-ome?"

"Eeeeeeekkkkk!!" came a scream from inside Beaver's house. "A snake! A huge snake! A monstrous talking snake! He'll kill us all!"

Then another voice called out: "I'll save you, Mrs. Beaver! I'll save you, my darling! Watch out you horrible snake — here I come!"

"Ow! Ow! Ouch!" squealed Ompliant, quickly pulling his trunk out of the house and staggering backwards.

Pine Cone and Pepper Pot hung on tightly as Ompliant lurched and plunged about the marsh.

"What's wrong?" they cried. "What's happening?"

"My twunk! My poor twunk!" wailed Ompliant, waving his trunk wildly back and forth in the air. "Beaver's biting my twunk and won't let go!"

"Stop! Stop! Mr. Beaver!" cried the gnomes. "It's just Ompliant's trunk! He was only saying hello!"

Mr. Beaver stopped struggling and looked carefully at the trunk. Then he looked at Ompliant. "Oops!" he said sheepishly. "I'm sorry, Ompliant. I thought your trunk was a giant snake! I hope I didn't bite you too badly!" and he let go of the trunk and splashed into Soggy Mire.

"It hurts!" moaned Ompliant. "It hurts badly!"

"Let's see," said Pine Cone and Pepper Pot, running down the trunk to see how badly he was hurt.

Ompliant held his trunk still while the gnomes looked at it carefully.

"It's okay," said Pine Cone. "It's only a little scratch. Lucky you have such thick skin—Mr. Beaver has very sharp teeth!"

"Oh, it hurts!" groaned Ompliant. "I'll never use my twunk again!"

"Yes, you will," soothed Pepper Pot. "It's only a little bite for such a big person like you."

Just then Mrs. Beaver stuck her head out of the water.

"Oh, dear!" she said, looking shocked. "It's only Ompliant. You should always knock at a beaver's house, Ompliant—especially if part of you looks like a snake!"

"Oh, my poor twunk," groaned Ompliant. "I'll never be the same! I'm ruined forever!"

"Nonsense," said Mrs. Beaver. "Let me see."

Ompliant stretched out his trunk and showed her his bite. She took one look at it, and shouted: "Mr. Beaver! Come here this instant!"

Mr. Beaver came over with his head hanging down.

"Look at this," she scolded. "All that fighting, and you only made one tiny scratch! You should be ashamed of yourself! I hope a real snake never comes into our house! Now go and get some rushes and mud."

So Mr. Beaver collected rushes and mud, and Mrs. Beaver put the cool mud onto Ompliant's trunk and wrapped it up with the rushes.

"Ah!" sighed Ompliant. "That feels better."

"So why are you visiting?" asked Mr. Beaver.

"We're making one table and three chairs for Tiptoes' birthday," said Pine Cone. "We found the perfect branch to make them, but it's much too far to drag home. We thought you could help because you know about wood."

"Where is it?" he asked.

"Way over by the ash grove that-a-way," said Pepper Pot, pointing into the forest.

"That's too far from Soggy Mire," said Mr. Beaver. "We beavers never go far from water—it's too dangerous. Why don't you ask Chips the Woodpecker. He knows about wood too."

"That's a good idea!" agreed the gnomes, and off they went.

6
The Branch is Not Good Food

Ompliant and the gnomes walked for a long time. Every now and then Ompliant stopped, flapped his huge ears, and listened. At last he said, "My ears are telling me things, Pine Cone and Pepper Pot."

"What are they telling you?" asked the gnomes.

"They're telling me Chips the Woodpecker is over that-a-way," he replied, pointing with his trunk, and off he lumbered.

In a little while the gnomes heard Chips hammering on a tree.

"There you are, Mr. Chips," said Pepper Pot when they found him. "We've been looking for you everywhere."

"Hammer, hammer," said Mr. Chips, knocking on the tree and sending wood chips flying. "How can I help you?"

"We're making one table and three chairs for Tiptoes Lightly, and we've found the perfect branch," replied Pepper Pot.

"But it's too far for us to drag home," added Pine Cone. "You know about wood. What shall we do?"

"Where is it?" asked Chips.

"Way over that-a-way by the ash grove," replied Pepper Pot, pointing into the forest.

So off Chips flew to the ash grove. They waited a long time, but at last he came back.

"I found it," said Chips. "I tested it for woodworms and wood bugs. It doesn't have any at all—not even one! That piece of wood is no good for a house—and certainly not for a table. The best wood is really rotten and full of bugs and worms. That way you can have dinner without even leaving your nest."

"But we don't want it rotten!" exclaimed Pepper Pot. "And besides, we wanted you to see how we might get it home."

"I don't know about that," answered Chips. "It's too big for me to fly with, that's for sure. Why don't you ask Dotted Owl—I saw him earlier over that-a-way," and he pointed with his beak. Then he went back to hammering his rotten tree.

7
Dotty Owl

Ompliant and the gnomes trekked through the forest till they came to the House of Dotted Owl. He lived in the hollow of a tree that Chips had hammered especially for him. His very best friends, and those who knew him well, called him 'Dotty' for short—but everybody else called him 'Mr. Dotted Owl' out of respect for his great wisdom.

"Whoo? Whoo? Whoo?" hooted Dotted Owl when he saw them coming.

"It's Pine Cone and Pepper Pot and Ompliant," they replied.

"I know *that*!" said Dotted Owl, sounding a little annoyed. "But *whoo* are you coming?"

"He means *why* are we coming," whispered Pine Cone into Pepper Pot's ear, remembering that dotted owls can only say 'whoo', and not 'why', or 'what', or 'where'.

"We're making Tiptoes Lightly one table and three chairs," answered Pepper Pot. "We found the perfect branch by the ash grove, but it's too far to bring home."

"Whoo, whoo," hooted Dotted Owl. "That is a most interesting question. Let's go look at it," and off they went.

They found the branch lying just where they left it. They saw where Chips had pecked at it to try to find bugs, but the wood was sound and only the bark had a few little holes in it.

"Yes, that is a good branch of wood," said Mr. Dotted Owl wisely.

"It is," agreed Pine Cone, "but how are we to get it home?"

"That is a perfect piece of wood for one table and three chairs," added Dotted Owl, looking at it carefully. "Especially for a little fairy whoo lives in an acorn."

"We know that too," said Pepper Pot.

"But how are you going to get it home?" asked Dotted Owl. "It's much too far to bring to your house."

"We don't know!" said Pepper Pot, getting exasperated. "That's why we came to ask you!"

"A most interesting question," said Dotted Owl, scratching his head. "A most interesting question. Let me think," and he closed his eyes and sat very still.

Ompliant and the gnomes waited expectantly. Five minutes passed and he did not stir. Then ten minutes passed and he still did not stir.

"I think he's gone to sleep," declared Ompliant at last. "I can hear him snoring."

"MR. DOTTED OWL!" shouted the gnomes. "WAKE UP!"

"Whoo! Whoo! So sorry," hooted Dotted Owl, opening his eyes. "I was awake all last night and didn't get a wink of sleep……So whoo was the question?……I seem to have forgotten."

"How are we supposed to get this branch home?" cried the gnomes.

"Ah, yes! Whoo whoo is to get the branch home?" he said. "I see…I see…Now let me think," and he closed his eyes again.

"This is silly," said Ompliant. "I'm tired of trying to find out who is supposed to bring this branch home. I'm going to do it myself," and he picked up the branch with his trunk and brought it back to the gnome's home.

8
The Table and Chairs are Drawn

The next morning Pine Cone and Pepper Pot looked carefully at their branch. They stroked it with their hands to feel its shape. They knocked and tapped it all over to hear if it was sound and firm. They even sniffed it with their noses to see if there was the tiniest bit of rot — and there wasn't. The wood was whole and sound.

"First we'll make some drawings," said Pepper Pot, patting the branch. "I'll draw the chairs and you draw the table."

So they sharpened their pencils and took out their drawing pads. Soon they had a set of drawings. The chairs were beautifully shaped with four slim legs each. The table was round and had five legs — Pine Cone wanted to make sure it would not fall over when the wind blew Tiptoes' acorn house back and forth.

The gnomes admired their work for a while, then rolled up the drawings and went to the House of the Carpenter Ants. They lived in a fallen-down tree on the sunny side of a hill not far from the edge of the forest.

"Knock! Knock!" went the gnomes when they reached the fallen-down tree. "Knock! Knock!"

But nobody replied.

"Perhaps they think we're woodpeckers come for lunch," said Pine Cone. "Woodpeckers always knock first."

So Pepper Pot reached over with a little stick, and went tap-tap-tap!

But still nobody replied.

"Perhaps they think we're little birds," said Pine Cone. "They tap-tap the trees when looking for bugs. What are we going to do?"

"Let's call them out," suggested Pepper Pot, and he chanted his Ant-Calling Song:

> *"Carpenter Ants*
> *In this old dead tree,*
> *Out you come*
> *On the count of three –*
> *One! Two!* ***Three!***"

Out came the ants by the hundreds and thousands. They were big ants. Some were black, some were dark brown, and some of them had wings. Last of all came the Ant Queen. She was extra big, with short, glossy brown wings.

"What do you want, Master Gnomes?" she asked in a queenly voice. "Why did you call us out here?"

"We're Pine Cone and Pepper Pot the gnomes," they said, introducing themselves. "We need carpenters to help us make one table and three chairs for Tiptoes Lightly—it's her birthday soon," and they held up their drawings.

"For Tiptoes Lightly!" exclaimed the Ant Queen. "She's our friend! Of course you can have some carpenters," and she called one hundred of her best ants.

"You go help these two gnomes," she commanded. "And make sure you mind your manners!"

"Thank you, Madam Ant Queen," said the gnomes gratefully, bowing low to the ground. They were delighted to have so many carpenters.

"You are most welcome," replied the Ant Queen. Then she turned and went back inside her house.

9

The Branch is Chewed

Pine Cone and Pepper Pot marched with the ants back to their pine tree. They spread the drawings onto the ground and the ants swarmed over them. Suddenly the ants started eating them up.

"Hey!" cried Pepper Pot. "Our beautiful drawings!"

"That's okay," said Pine Cone. "Maybe it's their way of getting the plans inside them."

Pine Cone and Pepper Pot sat down to watch. Sure enough, as soon as the drawings were eaten the ants set to work. First they clambered all over the branch and chewed at the bark until it was gone. Then they held a little pow-wow and went back to work again. They chewed and chewed, and little by little the table and chairs appeared out of the wood.

After a while one of the ants came up to the gnomes. "We're getting hungry and thirsty," he said.

"We have some honey," offered Pine Cone.

"And we can also make tea," added Pepper Pot.

"Yes, please!" said the ant. "We love honey and tea!"

So the gnomes ran inside and soon came out with two saucers—one filled with golden honey and the other with sweet tea.

"Honey and tea!" cried the ants, milling around excitedly, and in no time at all the honey and tea were gone, down to the last drop. Then they went back to work, chewing and chewing and chewing the wood.

The sun was low in the sky when they finished. There on the forest floor sat one table and three chairs. They were perfect and did not have a single joint or crack.

"Thank you!" cried the gnomes when they saw what a beautiful job the ants had done. "Tiptoes Lightly will love them!"

"You're welcome," replied the ants, and they marched back home through the darkening forest.

10
Pepper Pot is Flyed

A few days later the gnomes decided it was time to weave the seats and backs of the chairs. "We need a good weaver," said Pine Cone.

"The best there is," agreed Pepper Pot, nodding his head up and down.

"Let's ask Spinalot the Spider," suggested Pine Cone. "He's the best weaver in the forest."

So they picked up the three chairs and carried them to the House of Spider.

"Spin! Spin!" said Spinalot when he saw them coming. "What have you got there?"

"Three chairs for Tiptoes Lightly," replied the gnomes. "It's her birthday soon and the seats and backs need to be woven most beautifully."

"Tiptoes Lightly!" exclaimed Spinalot. "She's my friend! Of course I'll spin for her!"

So Pine Cone and Pepper Pot put the chairs down and Spinalot wove the most beautiful and delicate webs he had ever made.

"All finished!" he said when they were done.

"Oh, they look so fine!" said Pine Cone, admiring them.

"They're gorgeous!" declared Pepper Pot. "They look so sittable!" and he went to sit down on one of them.

"Stop!" cried Spinalot. "The webs are fresh!"

Too late! Pepper Pot had already sat down.

"What's wrong?" he asked, looking puzzled. "This chair is very comfy. I could sit here all day."

"You *will* be sitting there all day!" groaned Spinalot. "Fresh spider webs are sticky—that's how we catch flies! You won't be able to get up!"

Pepper Pot tried to stand up, but he couldn't—he was stuck to the chair like a fly!

"Oh, no!" groaned Pine Cone. "Pepper Pot is flyed! What do we do now?"

11
Pepper Pot is Pulled

Pine Cone and Spinalot tried to pull Pepper Pot out of the chair. They pulled him by his arms, and they pulled him by his legs—they even pulled him by his beard—but it was no use. He was stuck fast.

"You're stuck!" said Pine Cone.

"I know that!" grumped Pepper Pot, looking very annoyed.

He tried to get up, but toppled over onto the ground. Then he looked really silly, sitting on a chair and lying on the ground at the same time. Pine Cone and Spinalot had to work hard to get him up again.

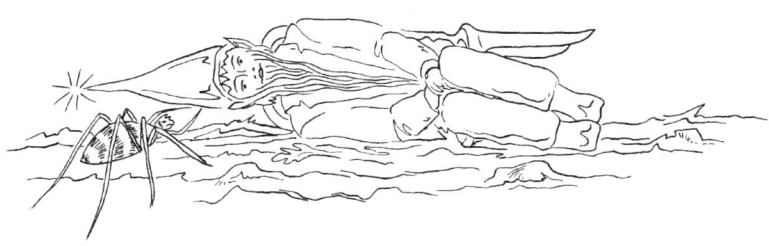

"You'll have to stay here in the forest," said Pine Cone. "We can't get you home."

"How long will I be stuck?" asked Pepper Pot.

"A week … or two," Spinalot replied, "maybe even three. I make the best and stickiest webs hereabouts. They can last for ages." Spinalot was proud of his webs.

"I'll get Jeremy Mouse," said Pine Cone at last. "Maybe he can help," and off he ran.

12
Jeremy Mouse is Called

"Jeremy Mouse! Jeremy Mouse!" cried Pine Cone when he reached the Mouse's house. Jeremy Mouse lived underneath the roots of the same great oak tree as Tiptoes Lightly. He was married to Jemima Mouse and they had five mouslings.

"Jeremy Mouse! Jeremy Mouse!" called Pine Cone, hammering on his door. "Come quickly! Pepper Pot is stuck to a chair and we can't get him off."

Jeremy Mouse came rushing out. "Pepper Pot is stuck! How did he get stuck?"

"We're making chairs," explained Pine Cone, "and Spinalot the Spider spun the webs for the seats and backs. Pepper Pot sat down on one while the webs were sticky and now he's stuck for weeks!"

"Let's get Tiptoes," said Jeremy Mouse. "She'll know what to do."

"We can't," groaned Pine Cone. "The chairs are for her birthday—they're a surprise."

"Oh, dear!" said Jeremy Mouse. "I'd better come quickly!" and off they ran to the forest.

13
Pepper Pot is Tree-Pulled

"Holy whiskers!" exclaimed Jeremy Mouse when he saw Pepper Pot sitting on the chair in the middle of the forest. "By my tail! Is he really stuck?"

"Yes, I am!" grumped Pepper Pot. "I'm stuck really good!"

"He's stuck really, *really* good," added Spinalot the Spider, sounding a little bit proud of how well his web was working.

"Let's pull," suggested Jeremy Mouse. "Perhaps he'll come off."

"We tried pulling," said Pine Cone. "It didn't work."

"Have you tried the tree hugging trick?" asked Jeremy Mouse. "Sometimes that works in bad cases of stuckness."

"No, we haven't," said Spinalot. "We should try that one."

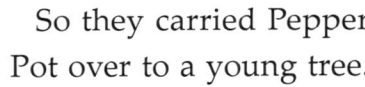

So they carried Pepper Pot over to a young tree. He put his arms and legs around it and hugged tight. Then Pine Cone grabbed the back of the chair, and Jeremy Mouse grabbed the tail of Pine Cone's jacket, and Spinalot grabbed Jeremy Mouse's tail, and they pulled and they pulled and they pulled. They pulled so hard that the tree bent right over—but Pepper Pot stayed stuck.

"My web is just too good," declared Spinalot. "What are we going to do?"

"He can't stay here in the forest for weeks," said Pine Cone. "We need somebody who can cut him free. That's the only way."

"I can chew the webbing off," said Jeremy Mouse. "I've got strong teeth."

"Your teeth are much too big," said Pepper Pot. "You'll either bite my behind or ruin the chair!"

"How about Annoyetta the Horsefly," suggested Spinalot. "She's got a very sharp mouth—just like a pair of scissors."

"That's a good idea," said Pine Cone. "But she lives in Farmer John's barn. We'll have to take Pepper Pot there."

So they picked Pepper Pot up and, bumpety-bump, carried him off to the barn.

14
Annoyetta is Found

Through the forest and over the fields they carried Pepper Pot to Farmer John's barn. It was a long way, but at last they reached the barn door. Luckily it was ajar—the door was much too big for them to open—and they went inside. The barn was cool and dim, and very big.

"I wonder where the House of Horsefly is?" asked Pine Cone.

"The House of Horsefly *is* the barn," said Jeremy Mouse. "This is where she lives."

"How will we find her?" asked Spinalot. "We could be looking for ages."

"Let's ask Chiron," suggested Jeremy Mouse. "He's a horse, or at least a pony, and I'm sure he'll know where she is."

"We'll have to be careful asking him about a horsefly," said Pine Cone. "Horseflies bite horses; they don't like them at all!"

So up and down the barn they wandered looking for Chiron's stall.

"Here he is!" said Pine Cone when they found him, and he climbed up the stall door.

Chiron looked at him with huge brown eyes.

"Good afternoon, little gnome," he said.

"Good afternoon, Chiron," replied Pine Cone in his most polite voice. "My name is Pine Cone and we have a problem."

"We?" said Chiron, looking at him carefully. "I only see one of you."

"The rest of us are down there," replied Pine Cone, pointing to the other side of the door.

Chiron looked over the stall door and saw one spider, one field mouse, and one Pepper Pot sitting on a chair. "That chair looks very comfy," he said.

"It is comfy, and it isn't comfy," replied Pepper Pot. "It's nice to sit on, but I'm stuck to it."

"Neigh!" snorted Chiron. "That couldn't be so!"

"It could be so, and it is so!" grumped Pepper Pot, and he tried to get up to show Chiron how stuck he really was, but only fell over again.

"You *are* stuck!" exclaimed Chiron with a whinny. "Well, well! But what can I do about it?"

"We need somebody who is very small, and with a mouth as sharp as scissors," explained Pine Cone. "That small somebody will be able to cut Pepper Pot out of the chair without damaging it. But we can't find that small somebody anywhere—though we do know that she lives here in the barn."

"But why did you come to me?" asked Chiron. "I'm not small, and I don't have teeth like sharp scissors."

"Yes," said Pine Cone, "but we are sure that the little, buzzing somebody lives around here. We thought you might know where that little buzzing somebody is."

"You don't mean that pesky, razor-toothed, Annoyetta the Horsefly do you?" snorted Chiron, stamping his feet and swishing his tail back and forth.

"She's the only one who can help," said Pine Cone nervously. "We thought she'd be around here somewhere."

"She *is* around here somewhere," snorted Chiron again, banging his hoofs against the walls. "How many times she has bitten me I do not know! Only this morning she bit my leg while I was snoozing! She's a lily-livered, sneaky, horrible little nuisance! If I ever get hold of her I'll… I'll…"

"We know you don't like horseflies," pleaded Pine Cone, "but we have to get Pepper Pot out of the chair without damaging it. It's for Tiptoes' birthday."

"For Tiptoes Lightly!" exclaimed Chiron. "That's a different story! Why didn't you tell me—she's my friend!" and he lifted his head and neighed loudly.

"Neigh! Neigh!" he called. "Come here, Annoyetta Horsefly! Chiron's calling you!"

Then he stood still and listened.

Soon they heard a loud buzzing sound.

"Zizzbizz, zizzbizz," went Annoyetta the Horsefly, zipping really fast this way and that over Chiron's head.

"This is a first!" buzzed Annoyetta, buzzing in a most annoying way. "I've never been called by a horse before!"

"It is the first time, and the last time, a horse will ever call you," retorted Chiron. "This here gnome is Pine Cone and he needs your help."

15
Pepper Pot is Snipped

Annoyetta the Horsefly landed next to Pepper Pot and looked at him with her huge multicolored eyes. She had a long, hairy body and shiny brown wings. She looked really strong. Pepper Pot also saw that her mouth looked like a pair of scissors. They had very sharp edges.

"Zizzbizz," buzzed Annoyetta looking at Pepper Pot. "That chair looks really cozzzy."

"It is," said Pepper Pot miserably, "but Spinalot the Spider spun the webbing and I sat down on it. Now I'm stuck."

"And what can I do about it?" buzzed Annoyetta, looking at Spinalot suspiciously. Annoyetta didn't like spiders one little bit.

"You have a sharp scissors-mouth," said Pine Cone. "You can snip him free without damaging the chair. It's for Tiptoes' birthday."

"Tiptoes Lightly!" exclaimed Annoyetta. "Why didn't you say so! She's my friend!"

Then she buzzed over to Pepper Pot, and snip-snip-snip, she neatly cut the strands of spider silk and Pepper Pot was free.

16
Wax is Thought of

Pine Cone and Pepper Pot carried the chair back to their pine tree and Spinalot spun a new seat and back. Then they went to spider's house to collect the other two chairs. Luckily nobody else had tried to sit down on them.

"These chairs are dangerous," said Pine Cone, looking at them seriously.

"Very, very dangerous!" agreed Pepper Pot. "They can't be left sitting around. We'll have to bring them inside."

"And make sure you keep your windows and doors closed tightly for at least three weeks," said Spinalot. "We wouldn't want any more gnomes, or even flies, getting stuck in the webs."

"Three weeks!" moaned Pine Cone. "Tiptoes' birthday is in three days!"

"What are we going to do?" groaned Pepper Pot.

"I don't know," replied Pine Cone, shaking his head. "It's late and I'm too tired to think properly. Let's lock the chairs in the pantry when we get home. I want to go to bed and sleep."

So they put the chairs in the pantry and locked the door — first making sure there were no flies or bugs inside. Then they went to bed.

The next morning the sun shone in their window.

"Good morning, Pine Cone! Good morning, Pepper Pot!" called the sun. "It's time to get out of bed."

Pine Cone and Pepper Pot got out of bed, washed their hands and faces, and brushed their teeth. Then they combed their beards until they were smooth and shiny.

Pepper Pot set the breakfast table while Pine Cone made toast and tea. They covered their toast with golden honey and sat down to eat.

"I know!" exclaimed Pine Cone all of a sudden.

"What do you know?" asked Pepper Pot.

"We still have to finish the table and chairs with beeswax. Perhaps the wax will stop the webbing from being sticky."

"That is definitely a good idea!" agreed Pepper Pot, nodding his head. "Let's try. We'll go to the House of Bee as soon as breakfast is over and see if we can get some wax."

17

Two Fine and Handsome Sailors

After breakfast the gnomes pulled on their red boots, gathered four buckets made from acorn caps and set off for Running River. The dew lay silvery on the leaves as they walked through the forest. It was still early, and the sunlight and mist played in and out between the tree trunks and branches.

When they reached Running River they untied their rowing boat. It had bamboo oars and a real name. They called it Skylark. Pine Cone and Pepper Pot had found it in a sandbox at Farmer John's house and dragged it all the way to the river. Then Pine Cone had painted its name on the back in blue.

They climbed into Skylark, pulled on the oars, and glided out onto Running River. The morning sun filtered through the rising mist and the water gurgled as it streamed through the reeds near the riverbank.

Now and then the gnomes heard the lonely, far-off cry of a loon.

Down Running River they drifted, sometimes gliding smoothly, and sometimes rocking back and forth on the waves. Soon the sun chased all the mist away and the sky became a clear blue dome high above their heads.

"I love being on Running River in the morning," said Pine Cone contentedly.

"So do I," agreed Pepper Pot. "It makes me feel so happy I want to sing and dance," and he jumped up and did a little jig on the end of the boat. He sang:

"Two fine and handsome gnomes are we,
 Jolly good sailors will we be!
  We'll shout and dance and sing a song,
   And step a jig as we drift along.

   Hey-ho! The diddle-di-doh!
    We'll step a jig as we drift along."

Pepper Pot looked so funny dancing on the end of the boat that Pine Cone burst out laughing and clapped his hands.

So Pepper Pot sang and danced some more.

> *"With pointed boots and trousers green,*
> *And tall red caps with tips that gleam —*
> *No smarter chaps you'll ever see,*
> *I know for sure you will agree!*
>
> *Hey-ho! The diddle-di-doh!*
> *I know for sure you will agree!"*

"Stop!" cried Pine Cone. "You're dancing too wildly! The boat's going to tip over!" He grabbed the sides to stop Skylark rocking, but too late — she flipped over with a lurch!

"Help!" cried Pepper Pot as he flew through the air.

"Splash!" went Pine Cone as he fell into the water.

"Silly gnomes!" grumbled Skylark as she floated upside down on Running River. "Now I might sink!"

Pepper Pot thrashed about as he tried to catch up with Skylark floating down the river. He reached her at last, grabbed hold of the front and swam for shore.

"Pine Cone! Pine Cone! Where are you?" he shouted — but Pine Cone was nowhere to be seen.

At last he reached a little beach and pulled Skylark onto the shore.

Up and down the riverbank Pepper Pot ran. "Pine Cone! Pine Cone!" he shouted. "Where are you?"

"Here I am!" a muffled voice replied.

"Where? Where? I can't see you!" shouted Pepper Pot.

"Under the boat!" said Pine Cone. "Turn Skylark over."

Pepper Pot quickly turned Skylark over — and there was Pine Cone, looking as wet and bedraggled as a soggy chicken.

"You look like a soggy chicken!" said Pepper Pot, trying hard not to smile.

"*I* look like a soggy chicken!" sniffed Pine Cone. "You should see yourself! You look like noodle soup!"

Pepper Pot looked at his messy clothes. His beard was all tangled up with weeds, broken reeds were hanging from his hat, and one boot was missing.

"I do look like noodle soup," he said at last, and burst out laughing.

18
The Bees Wax Generous

The gnomes searched up and down Running River for Pepper Pot's boot. They looked amongst the reeds and rushes, and even under stones, but it was nowhere to be found.

"It's lost," said Pine Cone.

"I don't feel like a proper gnome without two red boots," sighed Pepper Pot. "We'll just have to leave without it."

They pushed Skylark out into Running River again and rowed downstream.

"Lucky we didn't lose our oars," said Pepper Pot. "That really would have been a disaster!"

On they went over the waves till they reached the House of Bee. The hive was close to the shore in a hollow willow tree.

"Buzz! Buzz!" went the guard bees when they saw the gnomes coming. "Buzz! Buzz! What are you doing here?"

"We've come for beeswax," said Pine Cone. "We need it to finish some furniture."

"You'll have to ask the Queen," they replied, and went inside the hive.

After a while the Queen Bee appeared. She was huge for a bee and looked very important.

"Good day, little gnomes," said the Queen Bee. "I hear you are looking for wax."

"Yes," replied Pepper Pot. "We have to finish one table and three chairs for Tiptoes Lightly—it's soon to be her birthday."

"Tiptoes Lightly!" exclaimed the Queen Bee, looking delighted. "She's our friend! She helped the bee who lost his buzz! Of course you can have some wax—as much as you like," and she told her worker bees to fetch some.

"Thank you, Madam Queen Bee," said Pine Cone and Pepper Pot politely, bowing low to the ground. "That's generous of you."

Then they held out their acorn buckets and the bees filled them up.

19
The Boot is Found

Pine Cone and Pepper Pot rowed back upstream. It was much harder rowing against the current and soon they were sweating.

"I'm sweating!" said Pine Cone, wiping his brow.

"Me too," said Pepper Pot. "This is hard work."

All the way home they looked for Pepper Pot's boot—but there was no sign of it. Pine Cone even asked a fish who happened to swim past if he had seen it.

"Swish-swish," said the fish. "No, I haven't seen Pepper Pot's boot—but if I do I'll let you know for sure," and off he swam.

The sun was going down by the time they got back. They tied Skylark to a little willow growing close to the shore and walked home with the wax buckets swinging by their sides.

The forest was filled with twilight as their house came into sight. The moon had risen into the sky, and the gnomes saw an owl perched high in the branches of their pine tree.

"Is that Mr. Dotted Owl?" asked Pine Cone.

"It is!" agreed Pepper Pot. "I wonder what he's doing here?"

Suddenly Dotted Owl hooted very softly, "Whoo, whoo has lost his boot?"

"I have," said Pepper Pot. "I lost it when I fell into Running River."

Mr. Owl gazed at him with big, owly eyes.

"Whoo, whoo has found his boot?" he hooted.

"He's found your boot!" exclaimed Pine Cone, looking around.

Sure enough, there on the doorstep sat Pepper Pot's red boot, all dry and looking as good as ever.

"Thank you! Thank you!" cried Pepper Pot as he slipped it on. "Now I feel like a real gnome again!"

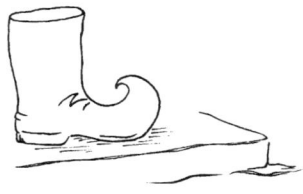

20
Pepper Pot Sits Again

Early the next morning Pine Cone and Pepper Pot took out their rag basket and searched for good pieces of cloth for waxing.

"Here's mine," said Pine Cone, holding up a white rag.

"I found one too," said Pepper Pot, holding up a bright yellow one. "Let's work on the table first."

They put the table in the middle of the living room on an old sheet. Then they dipped their rags into the beeswax and rubbed it over the wood. Soon the living room smelled of beeswax and honey. On and on they worked until the whole table was covered in wax.

They sang:

> *"Round and round with wax we go,*
> *Wax we go,*
> *Wax we go,*
> *Round and round with wax we go,*
> *Rubbing till the wood's aglow."*

Then they found fresh, clean rags and rubbed again. Round and round they rubbed until the wood was shiny and as soft as silk. They sang another song for this job:

*"Buff and burnish and polish and shine,
Polish and shine,
Polish and shine,
Buff and burnish and polish and shine,
On this table shall Tiptoes dine."*

"All done," said Pepper Pot, and he stood back to admire their work.

"It's perfect," exclaimed Pine Cone.

"Just lovely," agreed Pepper Pot. "Let's have lunch before we do the chairs."

After lunch they took one of the chairs out of the pantry and looked at it carefully.

"Let's use a very waxy rag," said Pine Cone, rolling up his sleeves and dipping the rag into the wax until it was completely covered. Then he carefully wiped the cloth over the webbing.

"See! It's working," he cried. "The cloth isn't sticking to the web at all."

Soon the whole seat was waxed. Pepper Pot touched it with his hand—but his hand didn't stick.

"Hurray!" cried the gnomes. "It works! Now the chairs will be ready for Tiptoes' birthday!" and they set to work again, waxing and rubbing and buffing all three chairs till they glowed warmly.

"Now for the final test," said Pepper Pot. "I shall sit on a chair and see what happens."

"Are you sure you want to try?" asked Pine Cone doubtfully.

"One of us has to," said Pepper Pot, "and I've had the most experience. We can't have Tiptoes sitting down on her birthday chair and getting stuck!" and he slowly sat down.

Pine Cone looked at him expectantly.

"Well?" he asked. "Is it sticky?"

"I don't know," said Pepper Pot. "I'm afraid to stand up."

He sat on the chair for a while, holding his breath.

"Okay," he said at last, "here goes!" And up he stood.

"The wax works," he cried happily. "I declare the one table and three chairs ready for Tiptoes' birthday!"

21
Off to the Great Oak Tree

Pine Cone and Pepper Pot woke up early on Tiptoes' birthday. The sun shone through their window and called, "Up you get, Master Gnomes! It's time to get up and about! Today is a special day as you must know!"

Pine Cone and Pepper Pot jumped out of bed and began to get ready. They were excited—Jemima Mouse had arranged for Tiptoes' birthday party to be a surprise.

The gnomes spent all morning brushing their hair, combing their beards, ironing their clothes and polishing their boots. Now it was time to go.

"Hurry up, Pepper Pot!" called Pine Cone. "We'll be late for the party."

"I'm coming! I'm coming!" answered Pepper Pot from the bedroom. "I'm just pulling on my party boots." Pepper Pot's party boots were extra red.

"All ready," Pepper Pot said, and stood in front of Pine Cone.

"How do I look?" he asked.

"Very handsome—for a gnome," Pine Cone replied, nodding his head up and down and smiling. "Let's get going!"

First they carried the table and chairs outside.

"I'll carry the table," said Pepper Pot. "Help me get it on my back."

So Pine Cone lifted the table onto Pepper Pot's back. Then he stacked the three chairs one on top of the other, hoisted them onto his shoulders, and off they went towards the great oak tree. Through the forest they hiked, then out into the meadow where the oak tree stood on its knoll overlooking Running River. They could see Tiptoes' acorn house hanging on the highest branch.

"I hope the others got Tiptoes out of the way," said Pine Cone. "It wouldn't be a surprise if she saw us coming with her presents on our backs."

When they reached the oak tree Jeremy Mouse came running out of his house.

"You're late!" he said. "Tiptoes will be back soon."

"You'll have to help us get the table and chairs up the tree," said Pepper Pot, putting the table down with a grunt. "We won't be able to do it alone."

"Okay," agreed Jeremy Mouse, "but we have to hurry!"

22

The Chairs are Hauled

Jeremy Mouse and the gnomes tried to get the table up the tree, but the tree trunk was too steep and the table too heavy.

"Oh, dear," gasped Pine Cone, beginning to panic. "We can't get it up!"

"Let's try the chairs first," suggested Jeremy Mouse. "If we tie them to our backs our hands will be free to climb."

So they gathered long meadow grass and tied the chairs onto their backs. Then up the tree they climbed until they reached Tiptoes' acorn house.

"That was easy," said Pepper Pot, admiring the beautiful chairs sitting in the living room.

"I have and idea!" said Jeremy Mouse, lighting up. "Why don't I tie the table to both of your backs. Then it won't be too heavy and your hands will be free to climb up the tree."

"Good idea, Jeremy Mouse," cried the gnomes excitedly, patting him on the head. "Let's go quickly—we don't have much time!"

23
The Table is Not Hauled

Pine Cone and Pepper Pot climbed down the tree and Jeremy Mouse scurried behind them. They went out into the meadow and gathered lots of long grass.

"Twist it into rope," said Pepper Pot. "It's much stronger that way."

So Pine Cone held one end of the grass while Pepper Pot twisted it round and round into rope. Then the gnomes laid the table on its side, put their backs against it, and Jeremy Mouse tied the table and the gnomes together.

"Make sure you tie it tightly," said Pine Cone. "We don't want the rope coming undone half way up the tree!"

"Okay," said Jeremy Mouse, tying it as tightly as he could. "I'll use the special knot Tiptoes taught me—she says it never comes undone."

Pine Cone and Pepper Pot waddled to the tree and began to climb up—but it was much harder than with the chairs.

"Work together! Work together!" encouraged Jeremy Mouse from the ground. "You'll make it."

"We're trying! We're trying!" called the gnomes—but they hadn't climbed very far when Pine Cone's foot slipped.

"I'm falling!" he cried, grasping wildly at the bark.

"Me too!" gasped Pepper Pot as they toppled backwards off the tree. Head over heels through the air they flew, their arms and legs flailing.

"Helllllp!!" they screeched.

The table landed feet first with a thud and stuck its legs firmly into the ground.

"Ooff!" grunted Pepper Pot.

"Ooff!" grunted Pine Cone.

"Oh dear!" squealed Jeremy Mouse. He ran over and found the gnomes lying on the table top, gazing up at the sky. "Are you okay?" he gasped.

"We th-th-think so!" gulped the gnomes when they got their breath back. "But you'd better untie us — we feel like a tortoise stuck on its back!"

Jeremy Mouse scurried underneath the table and tried to untie the knot.

"I can't undo it," he called. "It just won't come undone!"

"Try harder," said Pine Cone. "A knot must come undone."

So Jeremy Mouse tried harder.

"It just won't come undone," he moaned. "Every time I look at it my eyes go funny. Then I get confused and do the wrong thing. Tiptoes must have taught me a magic knot—that's what she meant when she said it never comes undone!"

"We can't just lie here counting clouds!" groaned Pepper Pot. "Do something, Jeremy Mouse!"

"What am I to do? What am I to do?" wailed Jeremy Mouse, running round and round in circles.

24
Ompliant Sort-of Helps

Pine Cone and Pepper Pot were fuming. Time was ticking by, and there they were, firmly tied to the table and gazing up at the sky.

At first Jeremy Mouse had tried to turn the table over, but its legs were stuck in the ground and wouldn't come out. Then he'd run off to get help.

"You should have brought rope," said Pine Cone. "Then we could have pulled the table up."

"You didn't bring rope either!" grumped Pepper Pot. "Why didn't you think of it?"

Back and forth the gnomes argued, and they were still arguing when the table started to tremble. At first it was just a little tremble, but then the ground began to shake like an earthquake. The gnomes tried to see what was happening, but the oak tree was in the way. Suddenly the shaking stopped and a huge head looked around the tree trunk.

"It's Ompliant the Elephant!" cried the gnomes, happy to see their friend.

Jeremy Mouse was perched on Ompliant's massive head. "I thought Ompliant might be able to help," he said.

"Hoo-humpf!" said Ompliant. "My ears have been telling me things."

"What things?" asked the gnomes.

"They've been telling me about gnomes again," said Ompliant, waving his trunk in the air.

"Which gnomes?" asked Pine Cone and Pepper Pot.

"Upside-down gnomes tied to a table," said Ompliant.

"That's us!" cried the gnomes together.

"So it seems," grinned Ompliant, flapping his ears back and forth. "You *do* look funny! I thought Jeremy Mouse was teasing me!"

"You have to help us," said Pepper Pot. "We're tied to the table with a magic knot and the table's legs are stuck in the ground."

"Hoo-humpf," said Ompliant. "So I see! I can do something about that!" and he reached over with his trunk and gently pulled the table out of the ground.

"There," he said, holding them close to one of his eyes, "you're no longer stuck in the ground."

"Thank you," said Pine Cone, "but we're still tied to the table."

"I can't help you with that," replied Ompliant, "but I will put you up the tree." And reaching as high as he could, he placed the gnomes onto the branch leading to Tiptoes' house.

25
Two Brave Gnomes and One Table

High above the ground Pine Cone and Pepper Pot were clinging to a branch of the great oak tree. Their knees were weak and wobbly. They were terrified.

"It's so far to the ground!" Pine Cone wailed, peering around the branch.

"Don't look down! Don't look down, you goose!" whimpered Pepper Pot. "Just hang on tight or we'll both fall down!"

Jeremy Mouse hurried up the tree and grabbed the table to keep it steady.

"We're not too far from Tiptoes' house," he said. "The worst part is over."

"Maybe for you," moaned the gnomes, "but you don't have a table tied to your back!"

"I'll keep it steady," said Jeremy Mouse. "If you crawl carefully I think you can make it."

Pine Cone and Pepper Pot crawled along the branch. Inch by inch they crept on their hands and knees, holding on for dear life. Higher and higher they went—but the further they went the thinner the branch became.

"This branch is getting very thin," said Pine Cone in a trembling voice.

"Very, very thin," agreed Pepper Pot, his knees knocking together with a clacking sound.

"You're almost there," encouraged Jeremy Mouse. "You can make it."

It took a while, and they had to be careful, but at last they reached Tiptoes' house. Jeremy Mouse opened the door and in they crawled.

"Phew!" said the gnomes, wiping their foreheads. "Safe at last!"

26
The Knot Knots

Pine Cone and Pepper Pot sat on their knees in the living room. The table was still on their backs and was beginning to feel heavy.

"I think it was nicer when we were lying on top of the table," said Pepper Pot.

"I think so too," agreed Pine Cone. "This table's beginning to feel heavy."

Jeremy Mouse was trying to untie the knot again, but wasn't getting anywhere. Every time he tried, his eyes rolled round and round in his head all by themselves.

"I can't see the knot properly," he told the gnomes. "My eyes just wander about in different directions!"

"Try closing your eyes," suggested Pine Cone. "That might work."

"That's a good idea," said Jeremy Mouse, so he closed his eyes tightly, reached out, and started to untie the knot. It came undone very easily—as if his hands knew exactly what to do.

"It's working!" Jeremy Mouse cried. "It's coming undone so easily!"

In a moment Jeremy Mouse had the knot untied.

"All done!" he sighed, very much relieved, and he opened his eyes.

But the first thing he saw was the knot—and the knot was *still* tied. The second thing he saw was his own tail lying in his hands—the end of it tied into a knot!

"My tail! My tail!" he wailed in surprise. "I tied my tail in a knot!"

"You what!?" asked the gnomes—they couldn't see Jeremy Mouse because he was on the other side of the table.

"The magic knot made me tie my own tail!" said Jeremy Mouse, showing them his tail.

"By my whiskers," gasped the gnomes, very impressed.

Luckily the knot in Jeremy Mouse's tail wasn't another magic knot and he soon had it undone.

"Thank goodness," he sighed. "I wouldn't want a knot in my tail for the rest of my life!"

Just then the door flew open and Jemima Mouse rushed in. She was carrying a birthday cake with one big candle in the middle. On the top, in beautiful mouse writing, she had written: *'Happy Birthday, Tiptoes'*.

"What are you *doing*?" she exclaimed when she saw the gnomes kneeling on the floor with a table on their backs. "Tiptoes is coming!"

"We can't untie the rope," explained Jeremy Mouse. "It has a magic knot and the gnomes are stuck!"

"Don't be silly," said Jemima Mouse. "Why do you think you have sharp teeth? Chew the rope off!"

"Yes, yes!" cried the gnomes. "That's a good idea! Chew it off, Jeremy Mouse!"

So Jeremy Mouse chewed the rope in two and it fell to the floor."

"Clean up quickly!" ordered Jemima Mouse, pulling the table into the center of the room and putting the cake in the middle. "Get rid of that rope and clean those table legs—they look dirty. Whatever have you been up to?"

"And straighten those chairs, too," she added. "I have to tell Ompliant to hide before Tiptoes sees him," and out of the house she ran in a rush.

27
Tiptoes' Surprise

Jemima Mouse scurried down the oak tree. She stopped on the lowest branch and looked towards Farmer John's house. She saw Tiptoes walking through the meadow towards the oak tree. With her were Pins and Needles the house fairies, Twiglets and Spriglets the orchard fairies, and all her mouse children.

"Quick, Ompliant!" she called. "Hide behind the tree before Tiptoes sees you."

"Okay," said Ompliant, and made himself as small as he could—which really wasn't very small at all—and stood stock still.

Jemima Mouse ran out into the meadow to meet Tiptoes. Here and there butterflies flitted above the grass and crickets chirped and sang.

"Hello, Tiptoes," she called when she got near.

"Hello, Jemima Mouse," said Tiptoes. "Look at all the people coming with me to the oak tree. It almost feels like we're going to have a party!"

"Oh, there's not going to be a party," replied Jemima Mouse, anxious to keep the party a secret. "It's just a beautiful day—that's why so many people are visiting. Isn't that so, Pins and Needles?"

"Yes, yes," agreed Pins and Needles, nodding their slim heads up and down. "Just a beautiful day!"

"Just a beautiful day! Just a beautiful day!" chanted the little mouslings dancing round and round them in

the grass—they had been told not to tell Tiptoes about her surprise birthday party.

"Your little mouslings are very excited today," said Tiptoes to Jemima Mouse. "They're full of beans!"

"Oh, they're always full of beans," said Jemima Mouse. "Isn't that so, Twiglets and Spriglets?"

"Yes, yes," agreed Twiglets and Spriglets with a curtsy. "Just full of beans!"

"And look!" said Tiptoes pointing. "What's Ompliant doing here?"

They all looked towards the oak tree, but didn't see anything.

"I don't see anything," said Jemima Mouse, puzzled.

"He's behind the tree," said Tiptoes. "I saw his ears flapping." Just then Ompliant flapped his ears again. It looked like the oak tree had grown strange wings.

"Oh, *that* Ompliant!" said Jemima Mouse. "Ummm ... yes ... he was helping Jeremy Mouse," she explained. "I forgot about that."

"Hello, Ompliant," called Tiptoes when they reached the oak tree. "Why are you hiding?"

"I'm playing hide and seek," said Ompliant. "You're not supposed to see me."

Tiptoes scratched her head. She didn't understand.

"Okay, Ompliant," she replied. "I didn't see you."

"That's good," answered Ompliant, "because I'm not here!"

"Why don't we go up to your house for afternoon tea," suggested Jemima Mouse to Tiptoes. "I hear the view is quite wonderful today."

"Yes! Yes!" cried the mouslings, "Let's go to your house, Tiptoes! The view is quite wonderful."

Tiptoes laughed at the mouslings. "Okay," she said. "Let's go up."

So up the tree all the mice ran, and the fairies opened their wings and flew after them. Pins and Needles kept Tiptoes talking till all the mice were inside the house. Then they opened the door and shooed her in.

"Surprise!" cried all the mice.

"Surprise!" cried all the fairies.

"Surprise!" cried Ompliant from way down below.

"What's this?" exclaimed Tiptoes, looking surprised. "A birthday cake sitting on a beautiful table with three gorgeous chairs. How wonderful!"

"Happy Birthday!" they all shouted.

"It *is* my birthday," said Tiptoes happily. "I thought you'd forgotten!"

Then everyone burst into a birthday song—with Ompliant singing the loudest of all.

> *"We wish you a happy birthday,*
> *A joyous and celebrated birthday,*
> *For our friend Tiptoes—*
> *May she live a long, long life!"*

"Thank you! Thank you!" cried Tiptoes, her eyes sparkling with happiness. "What a wonderful birthday surprise!" Then she ran to the window and leaned out. "Thank you too, Ompliant," she called, and blew him huge big kisses.

Ompliant was so happy that he raised his trunk high into the air and let out a huge elephant trumpet.

"Aaahhhhrrrooooooooooooommmmmmmmmm!" he trumpeted.

Far away in the fields Farmer John heard a sound he had never heard on his farm before.

"That sounds like an elephant!" he said, scratching his head.

"No! No! It couldn't be," he thought. "Not here on my farm!"

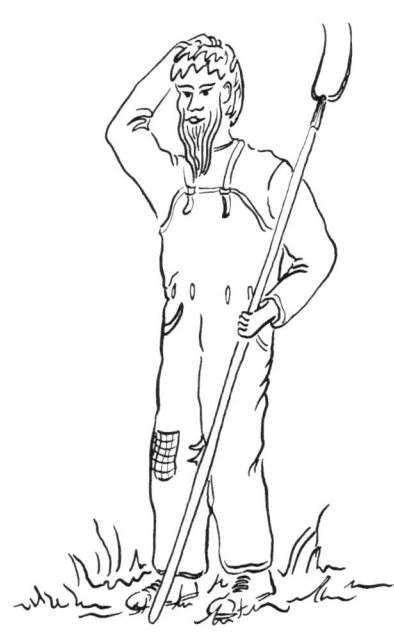

28
More Visitors

First Tiptoes blew out the candle and cut the cake. Everyone had a piece—even Ompliant—and they all agreed it tasted delicious. Then Tiptoes admired the beautiful table and the three gorgeous chairs. Everybody took turns sitting on the chairs—except Ompliant, of course—and said they were very comfy and cozy.

"This furniture looks so fine," said Tiptoes to Pine Cone and Pepper Pot. "They must have taken a lot of work."

"Oh, no! Not at all!" said Pine Cone, shaking his head.

"No, no! No work at all!" agreed Pepper Pot.

The gnomes were pleased at how much she liked her present.

"But how did you get them up the tree?" she asked. "That must have been very difficult."

"Oh, no, no!" said the gnomes together. "It was no bother at all! Ompliant and Jeremy Mouse helped us."

Just then the wind shook the house and rocked it back and forth.

"The wind! The wind!" cried Tiptoes, running to the window. "The wind has come for my birthday!" And she held out her hands in the sunshine and felt the wind on her face.

"You really do love the wind," said Jeremy Mouse.

"Yes," agreed Tiptoes. "She's my mother."

"Your mother!" exclaimed all the mouslings, surprised. "The wind is your mother? Then who's your father?"

"The sunlight," replied Tiptoes. "He's my father."

"Tell us how you were born," begged the mouslings. "It's your birthday and you must tell us how you were born."

"Okay," agreed Tiptoes, "but we'll have to go out and sit on the lowest branch so Ompliant can hear as well. He's still quite young—even though he's so big—and likes stories too."

So they all trouped out and sat on the lowest branch for Tiptoes to tell her birthday story.

29

Tiptoes Tells How She Was Born

"My ears are telling me things," said Ompliant when he saw them all sitting on the lowest branch of the oak tree.

"Yes," said Tiptoes, "your ears are telling you that a story is to be told!"

"Hoo-humpf! That's true," agreed Ompliant, flapping his ears. "You're going to tell us how you were born because it's your birthday!"

Tiptoes laughed and nodded her head. "Yes," she said, "now listen quietly."

"A long time ago the whole valley where this tree stands was covered with forest. The forest stretched as far as the mountains on one side, and as far as the sea on the other. One day the Sun was shining and the Wind Mother was dancing above the valley. Oh, how the forest loved the Wind Mother when her feet lightly touched the trees. Then the tree tops swayed and danced in her breeze.

But, deep in the forest, far down below the tree tops, there grew a little tree. It was an oak tree, not very old, with only a few leaves and one green acorn. It was much too small for the wind to reach because it grew in the shelter of so many big trees.

'Oh, Mother Wind,' cried the little oak tree, 'how I would love to feel your cool breezes on my branches. Oh, Father Sun, how I long for your light to fall on my leaves.'

The Wind Mother heard the little oak tree and plunged down into the forest. In and out between the tree trunks she blew, sending leaves scattering over the forest floor. She found the little tree, and round and round it she swirled.

'Little Oak Tree,' said the Wind Mother, 'I cannot always dive down into the forest, and the Sun Father cannot always reach you either. But we will give you a gift,' and she took the acorn in her hand and blew on it. In that moment a ray of sunlight shone down on the acorn too.

'From now on,' said the Wind Mother, 'a daughter of the sun and wind will live with you. She will stay in this little acorn and always look after you."

'But what shall I call her?' asked the little tree.

The Wind Mother pondered deeply. 'My daughter will be a child of light and of color,' she replied, 'and she will also dance as lightly as a breeze—I shall call her Tiptoes Lightly.'

Then the Wind Mother swirled away through the forest. Up through the branches she blew, passing away over the trees and herding the clouds like sheep."

"So that's how you were born!" exclaimed Jeremy Mouse, clapping his hands together.

"We like your birthday story!" cried the mouslings. "Is your acorn house that very same acorn?"

"Yes," said Tiptoes, "it is."

"Then it must be very old! This whole tree must be very old!"

"Yes, it is," said Tiptoes, nodding her head. "Far older than anyone knows."

"Then you must also be very, very old," said the mouslings in awe.

Tiptoes laughed. "Yes," she agreed. "I am very, very old!"

"But you look so young!" exclaimed Ompliant.

"Thank you, Ompliant," smiled Tiptoes. "I'm glad you said that! I am both young and old."

Then Tiptoes flew up into the sky, and round and round the oak tree she went, singing in the breeze and glittering in the sunlight.

30

Tiptoes is Told the Truth

The party was over and everyone had gone home—except for Pine Cone and Pepper Pot. They couldn't get enough of sitting on the new chairs.

"These chairs *are* comfy," said Pine Cone, wiggling just a little bit. "I can't get enough of sitting on them."

"They are so completely sittable," agreed Pepper Pot, wiggling just a little bit too.

Tiptoes sat in the third chair, smiling.

"I think these are the most sittable chairs in the whole world," she said. "But Pine Cone and Pepper Pot, if I look carefully, I can see tiny bits of dirt on the bottom of the table legs. Tell me, just how hard was it to get this table up the tree?"

Down below in the roots of the great oak tree Jeremy Mouse was putting his children to bed. Suddenly he heard Tiptoes laughing—and she didn't stop laughing for a long, long time.

The End

The Tale of None

The Tale of None

Once upon a time there lived a bug. She wasn't a big bug, she was a little bug, and her name was None. She was called None because she didn't have any spots—none at all! This made her sad. All her brothers and sisters (and she had many brothers and sisters) had spots. They had two spots, four spots, six spots, even eight spots, but she was spotless.

"Oh, what an unhappy thing to be so plain," she said to herself. "I wish I had spots – even just two."

Now, being spotless should not be *such* a problem – but it was. For this bug was a ladybug. Her head was just as black as all the other ladybugs, and her back was just as red. Indeed, she had a beautiful red back—as glossy and red as red can be.

"But what use is a beautiful red back if I don't have any spots!" she cried. "I wish I was spotty!"

So little ladybug None set out from home. She was tired of being teased and laughed at, and decided to find some spots for herself. Off she flew, over hills and plains till she came to India. It was a long, long way, but at last she came to India. There she met a spotted cow, with wide, wavy horns, huge brown eyes and large black spots on her hide.

"Ah," said the little bug to herself, "that animal has huge spots. Perhaps she will give me some of hers." So she landed on the cow's nose, and said: "O, Beautiful Beast of the Wide Horns! O, Mother of the Brown Eyes! May I have some of your spots?"

"Moo," said the cow, much pleased with such fine names. "Moo! Moo! Gladly would I give them to you, but they are much too big. They are so heavy that you would not be able to fly."

"But if I find two tiny spots may I have them?" she begged. "I will be able to fly with two tiny ones."

"Yes," replied the spotted cow. "If you can find them, you may have them."

So None wandered over the cow's hide, looking here and there and everywhere until she found two tiny spots hiding inside the cow's ear.

"I found some! I found some!" she shouted happily. "I found two tiny spots!"

"That's wonderful," answered the cow, "but please stop shouting so loudly. I can hardly hear myself chew!"

"I'm sorry, Madam Cow," said the ladybug in a very quiet voice. "I forgot I was inside your ear!" And she put the two spots on her back, thanked the cow, and went on her way.

She flew and she flew until she came to America. It was a long, long way, but at last she came to America. There she met a long-haired girl with freckles on her nose.

"Ah," said the ladybug, "what a beautiful creature. She has legs and spots just like me—she must surely be a cousin of mine. I will ask for some of hers."

So the little bug flew and landed on the girl's nose.

"O Long-Haired Creature of the Two Legs! O Mistress of the Spotty Nose!" she said, curtsying up and down. "May I have two of your nose-spots?"

"Giggle! Giggle!" said the girl, laughing because her nose was being tickled. "Of course you may have two of my freckle-spots."

So the little ladybug put them on her back, thanked the girl many, many times and went on her way.

On little None flew, her four spots glistening in the sun, until she came to Africa. It was a long, long way, but, yes, she flew all the way to Africa. There she met a leopard. She took one look at him, and exclaimed, "Oh, what a beautiful beast! He is so strong and fast, and so very, very spotty! I shall ask for some of his spots," and she flew to the leopard and landed on his nose.

"Dear Magnificent Lord of Spots," she said, bowing down low. "Dear Most Handsome Beast, such spots I have never seen! You have the finest spots that have ever been! O King of Spottyness, may I have some of your spots?"

"Purr! Purr!" said the leopard, very pleased with such a fine speech. "Purr! Purr! Yes, I will gladly give you two of my spots — one from each side of my back."

And that is why, no matter how often you count a leopard's spots, there are always two spots less than there should be.

Then the little ladybug flew home with her six spots shining on her back. There she was just like all the other ladybugs — except that she had a story to tell. Soon her tale became famous in Ladybug Land and was passed on from mother to daughter as 'The Tale of None'.

~ *The End* ~

A Note
On the Tiptoes Lightly Books

All the Tiptoes Lightly books are free-flowing adventures into the realms of wonder and magic characteristic of little children. Mostly sanguine and droll, sometimes reverent, or even spiritual, they are always on the lookout for fun. Lavishly illustrated (the drawings sometimes take more time than the writing!) they are innocent nature tales, suitable for reading to young children or for young children to read.

For the most part the Tiptoes' stories are based on my eurythmy lessons in kindergarten and grade one. The wonderful expressiveness of eurythmy, an art of movement and gesture using speech and music as its basis, lends itself to vivid, nature- and spirit-filled stories. In my lessons the tales were accompanied by live music which wove in and out of the spoken word and living gesture. Eventually they begged to be put down in written form. The first 'book', The Bee who lost his Buzz, was followed by six others, and soon thereafter a class teacher read them throughout the year to her first grade children with great success. The initial three 'books' are found in *The Tales of Tiptoes Lightly*; the next two, centered around the autumn and winter festivals, are published as *The Festival of Stones*, and the final two, centered around spring, are found in *Big-Stamp Two-Toes the Barefoot Giant*.

The Magic Knot, the fourth Tiptoes book, has only one story from the classroom—the one where Pine Cone and Pepper Pot upset their rowing boat and fall into the brink. The rest of the book was written because I enjoy writing for children.

Although Tiptoes was 'born' at the Monadnock Waldorf School in Keene, New Hampshire, the setting is, rather loosely, in California. This is where, following my stint in the east, I taught for five years at the Camellia Waldorf School in Sacramento. When I imagine Tiptoes and her friends they are sitting in the branches of the Great Oak Tree outside my eurythmy room, rowing down the

Sacramento River to the Pacific shores, or sailing up to the snow-capped Sierra Nevada mountains just visible in the distance. The little children often asked me as I passed by their playground, "Where's Tiptoes today?" or informed me, with the utmost seriousness, that they had seen her sitting in the flower garden, or that Pine Cone and Pepper Pot had definitely been spotted near the swings. And what wonderful smiles I got when they discovered that Pins and Needles slept in a pin cushion (how else?), and that you could so easily pass them by because they looked just like all the other pins and needles when they were asleep.

These characters took on a life of their own and, quite literally, populated the school. I have received many, many drawings of Tiptoes and crew, given to me for my birthday, or Christmas, or just 'because'. Which brings me to a secret I kept quiet about for quite some time: Tiptoes is real. Without her these stories could not have been written, or even imagined. Hopefully some of her magic has rubbed off on you and your children, and made the world a better place.

Reg Down, Sacramento, California, 2007.

P.S. Ompliant's name came from my eldest son when he was little. He couldn't say 'elephant' properly, so he used Ompliant instead. It's pronounced Om-plea-ant. ('Om' as in 'from')

Thank You!

I would like to thank all the parents and children—even adults without children!—who, through spoken word, emails, letters and drawings have been so generous in their praise for these books. An author hopes for kudos, but life teaches artists to be realistic and not expect too much. What I have received has been overwhelming, and heartwarming!

~ Website ~

For sample stories from

The Tales of Tiptoes Lightly
The Festival of Stones
Big-Stamp Two-Toes the Barefoot Giant
The Magic Knot ~ and other tangles!
The Lost Lagoon

please visit

www.tiptoes-lightly.net

Our website also contains additional stories for parents and teachers to tell to their children, as well as children's drawings of Tiptoes Lightly and crew. For teachers there is a fifth grade shadow puppet play, *King Sangara's Horse*, set in ancient India.

Printed in Great Britain
by Amazon.co.uk, Ltd.,
Marston Gate.